For **cat** owners who think they're in charge,
and the **cats** that know otherwise - SP

For my dog, Minnie, because I don't have a **cat** - EB

SIMON & SCHUSTER

First published in Great Britain in 2017 by Simon & Schuster UK Ltd 1st Floor, 222 Gray's Inn Road, London, WC1X 8HB • A CBS Company • Text copyright © 2017 Simon Philip • Illustrations copyright © 2017 Ella Bailey • The right of Simon Philip and Ella Bailey to be identified as the author and illustrator of this work has been asserted by them in accordance with the Copyright, Designs and Patents Act, 1988 • All rights reserved, including the right of reproduction in whole or in part in any form • A CIP catalogue record for this book is available from the British Library upon request • 978-1-4711-2412-9 (HB) • 978-1-4711-2413-6 (PB) 978-1-4711-2471-6 (eBook) • Printed in China • 10 9 8 7 6 5 4 3 2

I Don't know What To Call My Cat!

Simon Philip & Ella Bailey

SIMON & SCHUSTER
London   New York   Sydney   Toronto   New Delhi

I've got a new cat.

She just turned up on my doorstep one day
looking rather hungry.

She **obviously** liked my dinner
because she's stayed ever since.

It's fine. **I like cats.**

There's just one teeny, tiny problem.
I expect everyone with a new cat has it, but
I DON'T KNOW WHAT TO CALL MY CAT.

I thought 'Kitty' would be just right.

It wasn't.

Sometimes my cat can be difficult to please.

So I thought I'd call her Princess High and Mighty.

But she didn't seem keen on the dress.

I tried out

PAT and

Lorraine

TRICIA and **ETHEL**

tracey and

JANE and

Betty

Which are all lovely names . . .

I tried really hard to think of the best name for a boy cat.

Butch, Rambo, Arnie

and Rocky.

None of them were right.

But then I thought Mr Maestro was the perfect fit.

He seemed to like it too . . .

. . . until I decided to join in.

And **that** was the final straw.

Where did he go?

I looked everywhere.

But I couldn't find him.

Fresh

MISSING CAT
NO NAME

Not **even** at the zoo!

So I gave up.

There was nowhere else to look.
If only I'd been able to think of the right name.

'I miss my cat,' I said.

I didn't invite him to come home with me,
but still, my new pet's cheered me up.

And it turns out Steve was really easy to name.
Even if he was a bit moody at times.

Our days out together were lots of fun,
even when Steve was being a bit naughty.

Although I did sometimes have the strange feeling
we were being watched.

Everything was going perfectly until the day
we had some unexpected visitors.

I thought I might have seen one of them before.

It was a shame Steve had to leave so quickly.

BUREAU FOR NAUGHTY ANIMALS

BNA BNA

B·N·A

BANANA

But the **brilliant** thing was . . .

My cat came back! With a collar.

And a name!

TRICKY

Well, I suppose that fits. He was certainly **VERY** tricky to name.

I never did work out why Steve had to go.

But maybe one pet at a time is best for everyone.